GOLDILOCKS
and
The Three Bears

Illustrated by Andy Catling

 sequoia
children's publishing

Once upon a time, there were three bears who lived in a cottage in the forest.

There was Papa Bear, Mama Bear, and wee little Baby Bear.

One morning, Mama Bear made a breakfast of porridge. But the porridge was too hot, so the bears went for a walk while it cooled.

Soon, a nosy little girl named Goldilocks crept inside.
"I am so hungry," she said.

Goldilocks tasted Papa Bear's porridge.
"This is too hot," she said.
Then she tasted Mama Bear's porridge.
"This is too cold," she said.

Finally, Goldilocks tasted Baby Bear's porridge.
"This is just right," she said.
And she gobbled it all up.

Next, Goldilocks sat down on Papa Bear's
great big chair. "This is too hard," she said.
　　Then she sat down on Mama Bear's chair.
"This is too soft," she said.

Finally, Goldilocks sat down on
Baby Bear's wee little chair.
"This is just right," she said.
But she broke it all to bits!

"I am tired," said Goldilocks.

She found Papa Bear's great big bed.

"It is too tall," she said.

Then she found Mama Bear's bed.

"It is too wide," she said.

Finally, Goldilocks found Baby Bear's bed.
"It is just right," she said, and was soon
sound asleep.

The three bears returned from their walk,
hungry for breakfast.

"Someone's been eating my porridge!"
growled Papa Bear.

"Someone's been eating *my* porridge,"
said Mama Bear.

"Someone's been eating my porridge,"
cried Baby Bear, "and they ate it all up!"

The three bears went into their living room.
"Someone's been sitting in my chair!"
growled Papa Bear.

"Someone's been sitting in *my* chair,"
said Mama Bear.

"Someone's been sitting in my chair,"
cried Baby Bear, "and they broke it all to bits!"

The three bears went to their rooms.

"Someone's been sleeping in my bed!"
growled Papa Bear.

"Someone's been sleeping in *my* bed,"
said Mama Bear.

"Someone's been sleeping in my bed," cried Baby Bear, "and there she is!"

Goldilocks awoke. Startled, she jumped out of bed and leaped out the window, and the bears never saw her again.

~⊰❧ **The End** ☙⊱~

New Words

lock
(locks)
Locks in this story means "hair." Goldilocks means "golden hair." You don't open these locks with a key!

gobble
(gobbles, gobbled, gobbling)
To **gobble** something is to eat a lot of it fast. If you gobble up a bunch of candy, you will probably get a bellyache.

wee
Wee means really, really small. In the story, Baby Bear is called "wee little Baby Bear" because he is both young and tiny.

growl
(growls, growled, growling)
To **growl** is to talk in a grumpy way. Try it! Make a sound like an angry dog, then add words!

porridge
Porridge is a hot breakfast cereal, like oatmeal. Next time someone asks what you want for breakfast, say "I would like some porridge, please!"

bit
(bits)
Bits are teeny-tiny little pieces of something. If you break something to bits, you probably won't be able to fix it no matter how hard you try.

nosy
A **nosy** person wants to know all about other people's business. A nosy person would peek over your shoulder while you read. Better look behind you!

startle
(startles, startled, startling)
Startle means to surprise or scare someone. Creeping up behind your friends and shouting "Boo!" will probably startle them.

creep
(creeps, crept, creeping)
To **creep** is to hide and move quietly so nobody sees you. You might creep up behind your friends and shout "Boo!"

leap
(leaps, leapt, leaping)
To **leap** is to jump, but far and fast. Goldilocks leaps out the window at the end of the story, but you shouldn't try that at home!

Story Discussion

After you are done reading the story, think about what Goldilocks did and how the bears reacted. Be sure to look back at both the pictures and the words. Now it's time to answer these questions and talk about the story. After you read each question, choose the best word or think of your own.

1.) Look at the beginning of the story when Goldilocks first entered the Bears' house. How would you describe her actions?

Nosy   Curious

Forgetful   Something else?

2.) Look back at what Goldilocks did inside the cottage. Describe her behavior.

Careful   Rude

Funny   Something else?

3.) Look back at how the bears acted when they saw what Goldilocks did. Choose the best word for how each bear felt.

Confused   Upset

Angry   Something else?

4.) Look at the very end of the story. After the bears woke up Goldilocks, how do you think she felt?

Scared   Shy

Relieved   Something else?

·✾❧ Activities ❧✾· -

Goldilocks is gobbling down poor Baby Bear's breakfast! Can you spot 5 differences between the two images? (Answers on page 21)

If Goldilocks wrote a letter to the Three Bears, what do you think she would say?

Goldilocks
♥

To: The Three Bears
      Cute Cottage
      In The Woods

Dear Three Bears,

_____

_____

_____

_____

_____

_____

_____

♥ Goldilocks

Goldilocks follows a rule called The Rule of Three. This means things happen three at a time so they're easier to remember. There are three bowls, three chairs, and three beds. The porridge is too hot, too cold, or just right. And there are more! Start counting things that come in threes and you might be surprised. Some other stories that use the Rule of Three are *Three Little Pigs* and *Three Blind Mice*. Can you think of any others?

Goldilocks was made into a book almost 200 years ago, but it's even older than that! Before it was written down, people told the story to each other from memory. This is called a folk tale.

The star of *Goldilocks and the Three Bears* wasn't always a little girl. A long time ago, the story was about an old silver-haired woman instead. And in some of the old stories, Goldilocks wasn't a person at all. Instead, she was a fox!

The three bears weren't always a family. At first they were just Big Bear, Middle Bear, and Little Bear. One writer thought the bears were too scary. He made them a family so they would seem more like people, and they've been a family ever since!

Some scientists call a planet that is perfect for people and animals to live on a Goldilocks planet. It's not too hot and not too cold, but "just right." Earth is a Goldilocks planet!